BARRACK FIVE

ELYSE HOFFMAN

Copyright © 2020 by Elyse Hoffman
All rights reserved. No part of this book may be reproduced or used in any manner without written permission of the copyright owner except for the use of quotations in a book review. For more information, address: project613series@gmail.com

ISBN 978-1-952742-00-2 (ebook)

Project 613 Publishing
Project613Publishing.com

CONTENTS

Barrack Five   1

Afterword   47

Dedicated to my mother and father for their enduring support
To my grandfather whose stories I never heard
To all of the Rayas whose names were erased
And to God, Who makes all stories

BARRACK FIVE

Vilém Rehor had been dealing with graffiti since the day he was born. For one reason or another, some people felt the need to write their name or initials everywhere they went. Perhaps they were insecure. Perhaps they thought if they didn't make a point of leaving their name etched onto every wall, they would one day fade into obscurity.

Vilém had grown reluctantly accustomed to seeing signatures almost everywhere. On bathroom stalls, on desks in school, spray-painted on buildings, and once, while visiting the local courthouse on a civics field trip, he had even seen signatures scribbled on the walls of a holding cell.

But really, he thought with a frustrated shake of his head, *at a concentration camp?*

He couldn't say he enjoyed working at the Camp. Few people would, barring the overly enthusiastic historian or the odd sociopath, but Vilém, whose grandfather had once been imprisoned behind the barbed wire fence, felt particularly uneasy being stuck in such a place.

It wasn't a large concentration camp, certainly not the largest in the Czech Republic, but it had been the target of neo-Nazi attacks in the past. The Camp's director had thus decided a vigilant night guard was a necessity to prevent the fascists from destroying the terrible, precious history held within the barracks.

And that was his job. He patrolled the Camp all alone until 5 AM, when he could finally go home.

The Camp was a museum and memorial site now, but it wasn't like the polished-if-dreary Holocaust museums Vilém had visited in the past. It had a melancholic air to it, an ominous aura that made his skin crawl whenever he came to work. The curators might have fitted it with commemorative plaques and educational placards to give visitors information on the Camp's dark history, but all the denim-clad guests and golden plaques in the world couldn't banish the dreary ghosts that seemed to plague every corner of the complex.

Vilém hadn't thought being a night guard at a concentration camp would be like guarding an amusement park. His grandfather had never said much about his time in the Camp, but his silence had been forlorn enough for Vilém to know that the horrors he had witnessed in the barracks were beyond description.

He had only taken the job because he needed the money. Desperately. So desperately that he was more than willing to return to the Camp every night, even though the place made his stomach churn and his spine shiver.

But although the paycheck was his primary incentive,

Vilém had also hoped that working at a concentration camp would give him a reprieve from graffiti. The guests were normally quiet and respectful while touring the grounds. He had hoped they would respect the memory of the murdered Jews and refrain from leaving graffiti in their wake as they walked through the somber site.

So much for that.

He looked at the two words somebody had scratched onto one wall of Barrack Five.

RAYA POMNENKA

It was an unfortunate fact that teenagers were often insensitive and prone to vandalism, but Vilém had never encountered one as pompous and egocentric as Raya Pomnenka must have been. To be so thoughtless and self-absorbed, to deface a Holocaust memorial…

It was sickening, and although he hesitated to touch the barrack walls most of the time (they seemed particularly tainted by the sorrow that pervaded the rest of the Camp), he would have washed the graffiti off himself if he could. Unfortunately, the tactless teen that had defaced the barrack wall hadn't used a pen or marker. She had actually scratched her name into the wood.

The jagged letters stuck out on the otherwise blank wall of the barrack, and yet when Vilém examined the carving closely, he noticed that it didn't look like the average graffiti signature. The names he had seen written on past walls were almost always flamboyant and pretentious, with bright flashy colors and ornate bubbly letters to make them stand out.

This etching wasn't ostentatious at all. It seemed almost frantic, the way she had carved it onto the barrack wall. It looked like the last words of a dying person, one who was so desperate to leave a final message before their life was stolen away that they clawed it into the nearest structure.

If he hadn't known better, and if he hadn't been in Barrack Five just yesterday, he would have thought an inmate had scratched her name onto the wall during the war.

But just last night there had been no writing on the wall. It was far too fresh to have come from the hand of a Holocaust victim.

Regardless, Raya Pomnenka's name was now a permanent part of the exhibit. There was no way to remove it. It would be there until the day that the old wooden floors and walls of Barrack Five crumbled into dust.

THE NEXT DAY, AFTER THE last tour group left the Camp, Vilém made his rounds through the barracks to make sure that everything was in order and there were no straggling visitors wandering the grounds. He wouldn't want to lock some poor kid in the Camp overnight. Even he, an armed security guard, felt his blood congeal once the sun sunk under the horizon and the bitter night-time breeze began to blow through the grounds. A teenager trapped in the Camp would be terrified.

But then again, there was one particular teenager that he wouldn't mind locking in the Camp overnight: Raya Pomnenka.

The brat would definitely deserve it, he thought as he made his way to Barrack Five. *Maybe it would scare some decency into her.*

He entered Barrack Five and his anger at Raya Pomnenka tripled when he saw two more names carved beside the one he had discovered last night.

RAYA POMNENKA   RAYA POMNENKA   RAYA POMNENKA

Seriously? Vilém thought, grinding his teeth together in indignation. Once was bad enough, but the delinquent had actually returned to the Camp just to deface it even more? He would have to report this to his boss. They needed to watch out for a girl by the name of Raya Pomnenka and make sure she didn't enter the Camp again.

He examined the girl's graffiti and realized how fresh it was. He could see wooden shavings hanging off the final frantically-etched *Pomnenka.* He almost wanted to touch the letters, if only to sweep the shavings off the wall, but he hesitated.

There was something about the flimsy wooden walls that frightened him. The walls had been another prison for the inmates. They had been shoved into the tiny barrack and forced to sleep suffocatingly close to one another. They had wept for their lost families in the barrack. They had gotten sick in the barrack. They had died in the barrack.

Vilém didn't relish the idea of touching the walls that had once surrounded so much misery and death, but the letters Raya Pomnenka had carved...he almost felt as though they were calling to him. He knew they were mere markings, but still he felt his fingers twitch as the urge to touch the letters consumed his arm.

He raised his hand and swept the wooden shavings away. A frigid chill skittered through his body as his fingers brushed against the barrack wall. He pressed his hand against the graffiti and paused, waiting for some sort of epiphany.

Nothing happened. He sighed in disappointment. He wasn't sure what he had been expecting, but the desire to touch the letters had been so sudden and overwhelming that he had expected *something* to happen.

But as his fingers lingered on the letters, he suddenly felt drowsy. He blinked wearily and allowed his heavy eyelids to slide down.

Your name is Vilém, right?

Vilém's eyes sprung open. He pulled his hand away from the wall. It felt cold, numb, as though he had dipped it into a tub of icy water. He flexed his fingers in an attempt to get the frozen blood flowing again and glanced around Barrack Five. He could have sworn he heard someone speak to him. He could have sworn he heard a timid female voice inquire about his name.

Vilém shook his head. It was late, dark, and the Camp's foreboding atmosphere was getting to him. He needed some coffee and a nap.

Vilém's pupils flitted to the defaced wall and he felt

his hand tingle when he looked at the trio of *Raya Pomnenkas*. Narrowing his eyes at the girl's name one last time, he exited the barrack.

As soon as he was away from the etchings, his hand became warm again.

SIX.

When he went into Barrack Five the next day, there were six *Raya Pomnenkas* decorating the wall. How the girl had once again evaded security and carved her name onto the wall without a soul noticing was anyone's guess. Vilém had told his boss about the graffiti and was promised that the guides and guards would keep an eye out during the day.

But somehow or another, the little lawbreaker had made it into her preferred barrack and left behind three more markings for Vilém to moan about.

Had the girl been vandalizing something other than a Holocaust memorial, Vilém might have been rather impressed. She had determination, but that didn't change the fact that she was insulting the memory of everyone who had died in Barrack Five.

Not to mention she was getting Vilém into a hell of a lot of trouble. His job was to stop vandals from ruining the Camp's structures, after all, and even though he wasn't there all day, his boss still expected him to keep the Camp clean and safe from dark 'till dawn. Since the new markings didn't seem to show up until his shift, it was highly likely that Raya Pomnenka struck on his watch.

Because of this apparent fact, he stayed in Barrack Five throughout the majority of his shift. He figured that if the girl somehow managed to linger after hours and sneak into the barrack, he would catch her and all of this irritation would finally end.

Nobody crept into Barrack Five, however, and Vilém started to get bored and tired. He had been smart enough to bring a small coffee thermos since he didn't want to fall asleep on the job like he nearly had last night. The caffeine, unfortunately, was barely having any effect. Normally, he was rather jumpy during the late hours of his night shift, but now he had to struggle just to keep his eyes half open.

Once he finished the last drop of his coffee, his weary eyes started to roam about the tiny barrack until they finally landed on the offending carvings. Each seemed more desperate than the last. The *a*'s had been so hurriedly scrawled that they almost looked like *o*'s. He could tell the words hadn't been carved with a stick or tool of any sort. They had been clawed into the wood with Raya Pomnenka's fingernails. He had to wonder how her nails hadn't worn down or broken after scratching out her name so many times.

Vilém walked towards the letters. Without truly thinking, as if he were sleepwalking, he lifted his hand and touched the sixth *Raya*. His eyes instantly closed.

It is Vilém. I can see it right there, on your uniform. You're a guard here, yes?

He gasped and opened his eyes. That voice...it was the

same from last night. The same soft, worried female tone.

Vilém almost pulled out his gun, but instead he kept his hand on the markings. He scowled at the serrated script.

RAYA POMNENKA RAYA POMNENKA RAYA POMNENKA
RAYA POMNENKA RAYA POMNENKA RAYA POMNENKA

He pursed his lips curiously. *Well, no, it can't be.*

Vilém didn't exactly believe in ghosts, at least not the sort that they showed in movies. He didn't believe in translucent ghouls that could phase through solid matter and possess some poor character's body.

But he believed in spirits. He believed in them because he could feel them whenever he was in a place of death and sorrow.

When he stood by the grave of his grandmother, he could practically feel all of her regrets, the sadness she felt at leaving the world before she could do everything she wanted. When he visited Prague and stood where Reinhard Heydrich—the Nazi General who had ruled Czechoslovakia with an iron heart—had been assassinated by Czech agents, he could sense the German's furious spirit lingering at the spot where the heroes had struck him down.

And he sensed the mournful spirits of the Jews every night when he walked through the barracks where they had lived and died. That was why the Camp made him squirm. Not only because of what *had* happened, but because the unfortunate victims *still* seemed to be there, languishing over their lost lives.

Yet while he often sensed such grief-stricken spirits, he had never thought one would wholly remain in the place of its pain, that it would try to communicate with the living.

Maybe he was overtired. Maybe he had dozed off and was stuck in a strange dream.

But if that were the case, if this was just a dream, it wouldn't hurt to reply.

He inhaled and closed his eyes once more.

"Yes," he muttered under his breath. "My name is Vilém. I'm the night guard."

You're better than the last guard who was here.

He felt his skin become icy, as if the spirit carried the coldness of death with her, a coldness that clung to him as he communicated with her. He almost wanted to run out of the barrack and never return, but his curiosity kept him in place.

"Last guard? The one they fired or…are you talking about a Nazi?"

Vilém could swear he heard the spirit sigh.

Both, I suppose. The last guard here, the last Czech one, he always used to bring beer with him. Sat in the corner and just drank himself stupid.

"In a concentration camp?"

He wasn't a very good man. Not respectful at all. You don't seem so bad, though.

Vilém faintly recognized how odd this was. He was either having a conversation with a figment of his drowsy imagination or he was actually talking to a ghost, and neither option made him feel very good about his sanity. Perhaps he had been spending too much time in the Camp. It was driving him bonkers.

"Am I asleep?"

Your eyes are closed.

"I'm asleep, then. Good."

Good? Why?

"Because otherwise I'd be insane."

If you're asleep right now, you're a very talkative sleeper.

"I'm definitely asleep. You're in my head. You're not real."

There was silence for a moment. Vilém frowned.

"Hello?"

More silence. He thought he might have finally woken up. Yet as he stood there, with his eyes still closed and his fingers still touching the cold barrack wall, he could feel the gloomy presence close by.

"Hello?" he said again, softer this time, his tone almost apologetic.

I exist. I do. I exist.

The return of the voice made Vilém flinch, but his stomach sunk when he heard the spirit speak in a quiet and solemn manner. He had said something wrong, made her sadder than she already was. Even though he was still slightly dazed, he felt guilty right away.

He decided to end this conversation before something else went wrong. It was probably best not to tempt madness and mystic forces by responding to ethereal voices.

But just as he was about to open his eyes and take his hand off the barrack wall, the voice spoke up.

Please come back tomorrow and talk to me again. Please? I promise I'm real. I promise you aren't crazy. Please, I'm not going to hurt anybody, but I want to talk. Just try to talk to me tomorrow. Please?

The poor phantom sounded so frantic and frightened that he couldn't refuse. He gave a single nod and scurried out of Barrack Five. He figured that if she was merely a fantasy created by his fatigued mind, she wouldn't speak again.

And if she talks tomorrow...I guess I'm crazy, Vilém thought with a sardonic smirk. He considered himself to be of sound mind and didn't truly think he was going insane. His head felt fine, and he only heard strange things when he stood in Barrack Five. If his brain was on the fritz, surely he would be seeing and hearing things outside of the barrack. He wasn't, though, and thus he was almost certain that this was nothing but a drowsy delusion.

But there was a possibility that a troubled spirit was stubbornly clinging to Barrack Five, refusing to move on to the next world. If that was the case, he didn't think the spirit was a threat. She didn't feel like a malevolent force.

Still, his curiosity was aroused. He would get plenty of sleep once he got home so he would be wide awake for his shift tomorrow. Either the spirit truly didn't exist, or she would still be there, waiting to tell him why she refused to leave.

BARRACK FIVE

RAYA POMNENKA RAYA POMNENKA RAYA POMNENKA
RAYA POMNENKA RAYA POMNENKA RAYA POMNENKA
RAYA POMNENKA RAYA POMNENKA RAYA POMNENKA
RAYA POMNENKA RAYA POMNENKA RAYA POMNENKA
RAYA POMNENKA RAYA POMNENKA RAYA POMNENKA

Twenty-four. Before the gates of the Camp had even opened the next day, Raya Pomnenka quadrupled the number of times her name was scrawled on the wall of Barrack Five. Even the visitors had noticed the carvings, and several had asked their tour guides if some unfortunate inmate had made the markings during the Holocaust.

Vilém's boss was convinced that the Graffiti-Girl (as she had dubbed her) struck sometime during Vilém's shift. Suffice to say, she wasn't happy. Vilém was, as far as his boss was concerned, failing at his job. She assured him that he would face severe consequences if another *Raya Pomnenka* appeared on the wall.

Vilém, fortunately, was prepared. He had slept for as long as he could and arrived at the Camp just as dusk started to conquer daytime. He brought along a full thermos of extra-caffeinated espresso, as well as an emergency bottle of ice-cold water that he could splash himself with if all else failed and fatigue started to wear him down.

As soon as the last tour groups started to trickle out of the barbed-wire gate, Vilém scurried into Barrack Five and counted the *Raya Pomnenkas* on the wall. Once he was sure no new markings had been added to the barrack since his boss had scolded him, he sat beneath the graffiti and waited for the sun to slumber.

Soon, the sun vanished, the crickets started to chatter in the distance, and the wintry night-time wind made its way into the barrack. Vilém pulled his coat tightly around himself. He was waiting for a different kind of coldness to come into the barrack. The coldness that would accompany the anguished spirit once she arrived.

At last, he felt it. The eerie, icy feeling that only a woeful wraith could provide. He stood and looked around for some sign of the specter, but although he felt her presence, he didn't see her.

"Hello?" he called out. He waited a moment, but there was no response. His eyes traveled around the barren barrack for a moment as he searched for the spirit. Eventually, he looked at the twenty-four *Raya Pomnenkas* written up on the wall and remembered how he had communicated with the ghost yesterday.

He placed his hand on the markings and closed his eyes.

"Hello?" he said again.

You came back.

She sounded so relieved, as though her very soul had been at stake. Hearing the spirit while he was wide awake confirmed that she hadn't been a hallucination crafted by his erstwhile-exhausted brain. He cringed and chewed on his tongue, wondering how to respond to such an anomaly.

"So…" he muttered. "You were right. You do exist… that or I'm losing my marbles."

You're not crazy, I promise.

She sounded almost amused.

"Thank you for your assurance…ghost. I guess you were telling the truth before, so I'll take your word for it now."

The spirit didn't reply for a moment, and when she did, her tone was noticeably dejected.

Telling the truth about what? Existing? I've existed for a long time, but nobody...

Her voice drifted off. He winced when he felt her arctic aura distance itself, as though she was taking a step away from him.

"I didn't mean to upset you," he said. "I'm sorry."

He felt her cold presence creep close once more.

It's all right. You didn't say anything bad, not really. It's just me...

"I'm a…bit curious, though. How long have you existed *here*, at the Camp?"

Forever.

He might have raised an eyebrow if his eyes weren't firmly shut. "Forever? That's not possible."

It feels like it's been forever.

"Are you trapped here?" asked Vilém. "Do you need help?"

Trapped?

"Are you stuck here, at the Camp? Is there something preventing you from…well…you know…"

Moving on?

"Yes. To…whatever's next."

I don't think I'm trapped here. I think I could leave…but I can't.

"You can but you can't? Or is it more like you can, but you won't?"

The spirit was silent.

"I see," said Vilém. "Well then...I assume your name is Raya Pomnenka."

It is.

"That's what I thought. And you're the one that's been scratching your name onto this wall."

I'm sorry.

"You don't need to apologize. I thought you were some stupid kid, but I guess I was wrong."

Half wrong. I am a kid, but I'm not stupid.

He almost chuckled. The spirit's tone had become slightly brighter, and he definitely preferred to hear her soft voice when it was filled with mirth rather than melancholy.

"Well, young lady," he said, "I'll forgive you for vandalizing the memorial site if you'll please explain why you did so."

There was silence for a moment, yet he didn't feel her presence recede like it did when he said something wrong. He could tell that the spirit was pondering his request, deciding whether or not he was worthy of being answered.

Finally, Raya spoke in an almost hopeful manner.

Instead of telling you, how about I show you?

Vilém's brow furrowed. "Show me? How on earth will you show me?"

I'll show you what happened to me. I think you'll understand better if I show you. Just keep your hand on the wall and your eyes closed.

"Hold on a minute, Raya," he started to say, and he could feel a small surge of warm happiness radiate from the nearby spirit when he uttered her name.

"You want to get inside my head?"

In a way.

"I'm not sure I can do that, Raya. It's weird enough that I'm hearing ghosts. I don't think having one mess with my mind would be good for my health."

You won't get hurt, I promise. It's just my memories. I just...want to show them to somebody. Please, please, Vilém? Please let me show you! It's been so long since I've talked to somebody. I'm not sure I'll ever get another chance! Please...

She sounded almost frantic, as though the world would end if he didn't concede.

Poor girl, he thought. He wouldn't be able to sleep with a clear conscience if he refused her poignant plea. The girl's spirit was, somehow or another, stuck in the barrack, and it was his job to make sure that no children were trapped in the Camp. Perhaps if he watched her memories, he could figure out a way to free her troubled spirit, help her find peace.

"All right, Raya," he said, heaving a small sigh and bracing himself for the mighty headache he would most likely receive once he was thrown into the girl's recollections. "Go ahead. Show me what happened to you."

The transition from the dark, ominous interior of Barrack Five to Raya Pomnenka's memory was so fast and painless that it was almost startling in and of itself. One second he could feel the cold draft nipping at his nose, and the next he was in a warm bedroom with lavender walls, standing in front of a mirror.

But the reflection that looked back wasn't his own. Rather, it was a young girl, no more than nine years old. She had curly auburn hair that had been clumsily tied into two pigtails. An extended family of freckles was splashed across her beaming face. Her chestnut-brown eyes sparkled with excitement as she straightened out her bright blue dress.

Vilém was astonished. It was as though someone had tossed him back in time, right into the body of little Raya Pomnenka. Although he couldn't control what the girl did, he could see everything that she saw and feel everything she felt. He could feel the excitement that was bubbling in the girl's chest as she spun around and admired her new dress.

"Raya?" he called out.

Yes, Vilém?

"Oh, good, you're still there," he said as he watched little Raya giggle with delight and blow her reflection a kiss.

I wouldn't leave you.

"Thanks. So…how old are you here?"

Nine. This is the earliest memory I have.

"The earliest? At nine?" He could tell from the spirit's voice that she must have been a teenager, no older than seventeen, when she perished. She hadn't lived long enough to gain senility and lose most of her early memories. Vilém himself could easily remember many incidents from when he was a toddler.

Watch for a minute.

He obeyed and observed silently. Raya brushed a small lock of hair behind her ear and, apparently satisfied with her appearance, dashed out of her room. She ran down a hallway that was lined with portraits and family photos before skittering down the stairs and into the dining room.

"Raya! There you are!" laughed a stout woman with the same chestnut-colored eyes as the little girl. Vilém assumed she was Raya's mother. Mrs. Pomnenka kissed her daughter on the forehead and stepped back, smiling widely.

"You finally wore your new dress!" she cried happily. Raya nodded, pinching a corner of her dress and curtsying gracefully.

"Uh huh!" chirped the little girl. "I wanted to save it for the last day!"

"And speaking of the last day!" cried a man with a lampshade moustache and beady black eyes, no doubt Raya's father.

"Raya, sweetie, come here," said Mr. Pomnenka, stepping aside to reveal an eight-pronged candelabra.

"A menorah?" Vilém observed. His grandfather had never been pushy about his Jewishness, but he had possessed an impressive menorah collection. His menorahs had always been coated in wax, however, while the Pomnenkas' shimmered like new.

Yes, it is. This was the eighth night of my ninth Hanukkah, and Papa had promised to let me light the candles. I was finally old enough.

Vilém could feel Raya's heart race ecstatically as she scuttled over to her father. Mr. Pomnenka dragged a small stool in front of the table so Raya could safely reach the menorah. Raya hopped onto the stool and her eyes shifted to her father, her fingers tapping the table with impatient fervor.

Mr. Pomnenka lit one candle and handed it to his daughter. He almost grabbed her wrist so he could guide her shaky little hand, but she pouted and pulled away.

"Papa!" she whined, "You promised! By myself! I'm older now, I can do it all by myself!"

Mr. Pomnenka let his hand fall to his side. Vilém felt a pang of guilt shoot through Raya's stomach as she saw her father's eyes sparkle sadly. Slowly, however, an accepting but still somewhat despondent smile came to his face.

"Yes, Raya, I suppose you can," Mr. Pomnenka sighed. It seemed like he had just realized that his baby girl was no longer a baby that needed him to hold her hand at every moment.

"Be careful, dear," said Raya's mother, shuffling conspicuously close to the sink. "Fire is pretty, but it's also dangerous. If you don't respect it and treat it with care, you'll get burned."

Raya nodded, looking down at the candle and feeling a surge of pride, no doubt delighted that she was now old enough to handle such a powerful element. Carefully, under the watchful and somewhat frightened gaze of her mother and father, she used the candle to light the others on the menorah, spreading the light while her mother and father prayed in a lovely, familiar tongue.

"*Baruch atah Adonai...*"

"What are they saying?" asked Vilém. He could remember attending his grandfather's ceremonies for Hanukkah and Passover, but he had never learned more than three words of Hebrew.

Blessed are thou, O Lord...

"*Eloheinu melech ha'olam...*"

Our God, the King of the Universe...

"*Asher kidishanu b'mitz'votav...*"

Who sanctified us with his commandments...

"*V'tzivani 'lad'lik neir shel Chanukah.*"

And commanded us to light the lights of Hanukkah.

BARRACK FIVE

As he listened to the spirit's solemn translation of the prayer she clearly knew by heart, Vilém was almost tempted to ask her if she still believed in God. He could only assume that a specter stuck in a concentration camp had witnessed many horrors, perhaps enough to make her question the Creator's existence. Even though his grandfather had clung to his Jewishness, Vilém had always sensed that Grandpa Fabian's devotion was more to his people than to the God that had seemingly abandoned him back then.

He decided that asking about Raya's faith right at that moment would be insensitive, however, and stayed silent.

"Amen!" cried Raya, gazing proudly at the candles she had lit. The flames swayed to and fro, dancing gracefully in place, celebrating their temporary vivacity.

Raya turned around and curtsied once more as her parents applauded her achievement.

"Very good, Raya!" said Mr. Pomnenka, putting his hand on her shoulder and squeezing tenderly. "I should stop underestimating you."

"That's right!" chirped Raya, eliciting a chortle from her father.

"Well," cried Raya's mother, reaching into the living room and picking up a brightly-wrapped box that had been hidden behind the door.

"Since you're old enough to be responsible now, your father and I think you're ready for this," said Mrs. Pomnenka, setting the present at her daughter's feet.

"What is it? What is it?" squealed Raya, dropping to her knees and tearing the red bows and yellow paper to shreds. Raya opened the box and her eyes bulged in bewildered astonishment as she pulled out her Hanukkah present.

It was a large, bulky machine that Vilém barely recognized as a camera. The old contraption was nothing like the sleek devices that he was used to. It looked like a gray metal box with a giant lens stuck to the front. Raya's little hands could hardly hold the heavy object, yet the little girl gawked at the gadget with wonder, as though it was the most precious treasure in the world.

"A camera?" Vilém said as nine-year-old Raya jumped to her feet and hugged her parents, thanking them over and over for the gift.

I've always had a terrible memory, you see. That's why I have such trouble remembering anything earlier than this. After I got the camera, though, I could capture moments, memories. Then I didn't forget.

"Here! Let me try it out!" cried little Raya, lifting the camera and waving for her mother and father to stand beside the menorah. Her parents dutifully obliged and posed beside the golden candelabra. Raya fumbled with the camera a bit, trying to get it to focus and making sure that her parents were properly in the frame. Once the shot was perfect, she gave a small, satisfied nod.

"Smile!"

C*lick!*

A blinding flash absorbed the memory. As it dissipated, Vilém was surprised to find that the scene had changed. Raya was grasping her father's sweaty hand, and Vilém could feel small beads of moisture clinging to her brow. It was hot as a desert. The sun's brutal rays battered the father and daughter as they marched down a small pathway. Raya could feel her exposed flesh sizzling in the heat, yet she was too happy to truly care. She looked to her left and grinned when she saw a sign.

"*Lions: This Way.*"

"Come on, Papa!" she cried, pulling on her father's arm, yanking him towards the lion exhibit.

"We're at a zoo now," Vilém observed.

I grew up in a very small town. There weren't any big theaters or amusement parks, but there was a little zoo. Papa and I...we used to go to the zoo all the time.

Vilém realized that the girl's Hanukkah present, her precious camera, was lovingly tucked under her arm. Once she and her father arrived at the lion's cage, her father picked her up and sat her on his shoulders, giving her a good view of the lone lion that was lying on a small patch of hay.

"Nudný!" the girl cried to the creature, holding up her camera. "Come on, Nudný! Stand up! Pose for a picture!"

"Nudný?" repeated Vilém with a snort, recognizing the Czech word for 'boring' right away.

I named him that because he never moved. He was always lying down whenever I came to visit.

And the lackadaisical lion clearly wasn't about to change its stationary schedule for the sake of the little photographer. Raya released a disappointed sigh.

"Wow," she grumbled, glowering at the lethargic feline. "Nudný's real lazy. Papa, are all lions as lazy as Nudný?"

"Not at all," Mr. Pomnenka chuckled. "Nudný's just spoiled. Most lions are fierce and strong. They don't just lie down all day. The coat of arms for Czechoslovakia is a lion, you know."

"'Cause we're fierce and powerful?" asked the girl.

"That's right."

"Not 'cause we're lazy like Nudný."

Mr. Pomnenka laughed. "No, not because we're lazy like Nudný. Why don't you take a picture of him, Raya?"

"He's not doing anything."

"Well, just for posterity's sake. So in the future you can remember how lazy Nudný was."

The girl pursed her lips for a moment, no doubt pondering whether or not the sluggish feline was worth the film. She eventually conceded, however, and raised her camera.

C‌LICK!

With a flash, the memory dissolved and was quickly replaced with another. Raya stood in a dark little room, putting on gloves. There was a sink in front of her, and in the sink, there was a large tub filled with chemicals.

"Where are we now?" Vilém asked.

My developing room. I used to carry my camera with me wherever I went. I loved taking pictures. I loved being able to capture moments and keep them forever. Mama and Papa set up this room for me, a place I could develop my pictures. They helped me at first, but pretty soon I could do it all by myself.

Vilém watched as Raya carefully soaked a sheet of paper in the chemical tub. After the sheet had bathed long enough, she took it out and hung it on a clothesline where it could safely dry.

The memory dissolved into darkness.

"Uhm…" muttered Vilém when a new memory failed to fill the void. "So…what happened next?"

Everything you just saw happened in 1937. The year after that…

"The Munich Betrayal!" Vilém blurted. He hadn't been the best student in school, but he had paid enough attention in history class to know what that dreadful year meant for his homeland.

The Western Powers were as lazy as Nudný in 1938. Hitler asked for part of Czechoslovakia, the Sudetenland, and Chamberlain handed it to him on a silver platter. Mama and Papa were worried, but they didn't even consider moving. Papa said that Czechoslovakia was our home, and we couldn't let a maniac like Hitler drive us away. So we stayed, and we hoped that Hitler would be satisfied with the Sudetenland.

"He wasn't."

No.

Color came to the darkness and Vilém was thrust into another memory. Shouts and cheers assaulted Raya Pomnenka's ears as she stood on the side of the street, stuck in a small sea of adoring onlookers that hollered happily and waved little red flags as a troop of soldiers marched by.

Vilém felt his (or perhaps it was Raya's) heart go cold when he looked closely at the marching men. As they walked, they lifted their legs high into the air. Under normal circumstances, their odd and stiff strut would have seemed comical, but there was nothing funny about the black-clad men who marched through Raya's little hometown. Vilém knew who they were: minions of a madman, harbingers of the Holocaust.

"Those are SS soldiers!" Vilém cried, almost fearing

that Raya's spirit wouldn't be able to hear him over the din that the spectators were making. "Why are they cheering? This is a Czech town!"

It was. But there were also many Germans living alongside us. To them, the Nazis brought freedom.

"Freedom…" Vilém growled, glancing at the swastika-emblazoned flags that the German civilians waved with pride.

Raya Pomnenka bit her lip, gripping her beloved camera with both hands and watching the Nazis. Slowly, as though she was afraid that documenting this disaster would only make it worse, she raised her camera.

*C*LICK*!*

The memory melted away.

Raya could feel her father grasping her little hand. He was squeezing a bit too hard in an attempt to comfort her, and her hand was beginning to feel sore. But she didn't ask him to loosen his grip. She was too focused on the metal gate in front of her.

There were two signs hanging on the gate. One bragged in bright blue letters that this was the entrance to the zoo. The other showcased a proclamation in harsh gothic script:

*J*UDEN *V*ERBOTEN
*J*EWS *F*ORBIDDEN

Vilém felt Raya's stomach sink like a ship in savage seas. She stared at the sign for a few more seconds before her eyes traveled to a rigid Nazi officer that stood by the gate, inspecting the visitors' identification cards as they entered. His cold gray eyes flitted sideways, falling upon Raya. He scowled at her, as though the little girl that cradled a camera to her chest was an enemy soldier that he needed to keep at bay, and she shivered.

"Raya, sweetie," Mr. Pomnenka whispered warily. "Raya, we should go. Nudný probably wasn't going to move anyway."

"But he might have," she muttered somberly, wrenching her hand from her father's grasp, raising her camera, and snapping a picture of the "Jews Forbidden" sign. Vilém was startled when the memory didn't fade right away. Instead, Raya lowered her camera and grabbed her father's hand again, allowing him to lead her away from the zoo and the glaring guard.

"Will I be able to see Nudný again?" she asked her father.

"I don't know, sweetie."

"But I want to see him!"

Raya's father released a rather forced laugh. "You always complain about him! You always say he's boring and lazy!"

"He is, but I still like to see him." Raya looked down at her mud-encrusted shoes, loneliness settling in the pit of her stomach, weighing it down like an anvil.

I really did love that lion. Actually...I can't remember the names of any of my old friends or classmates. I remember Nudný, though. Poor Nudný.

"What happened to him?" asked Vilém as Raya and her father walked in uncomfortable silence for some time.

This whole town was bombed to smithereens near the end

of the war. Navigation mistake by some Allied pilots, apparently. All the buildings were destroyed, all the documents burned, and the zoo was obliterated. I think Nudný was killed during that bombings. Or maybe he starved to death before then. I don't know.

"Raya, look!"

Mr. Pomnenka's cry startled both Raya and Vilém. Raya's father seemed both astounded and elated as he looked at a graffiti-clad wall.

"What is it, Papa?" asked Raya. Her father placed his finger on the symbol that had grabbed his attention: a freshly painted "V."

"Do you know what this is, Raya?" he asked. The girl squinted and leaned closer, examining the "V" as carefully as possible, but she couldn't figure out what made it noteworthy. She shook her head.

"'V' for 'Victory,'" he said, the English word tumbling clumsily off of his tongue. "Or maybe it stands for '*ven.*'"

"Get out?" said Raya, standing on her tiptoes and trying to brush her hand against the smooth edge of the defiant letter.

"As in, '*Ven,* Nazis! Victory for the Czechs!'"

"*Ven,* Nazis!" chirped Raya a bit too loudly. Her father pressed his hand over her mouth and glanced nervously over his shoulder.

"Hush," he said once he was sure that no nearby Nazis had heard her outburst. "I don't want you to say something like that out loud, understand?"

Raya nodded timidly.

"Good girl. Not that I disagree, though. And this letter here, it shows that our people aren't going to put up with this. We won't let the Germans beat us down. We'll have victory."

He knelt before his daughter and gently tapped the covered lens of her camera. "Take a picture, sweetie. So you can remember the 'V.'"

An optimistic smile bloomed on Raya's face and she lifted up her camera.

CLICK!

With a snap and a blinding flash, the memory faded.

An abrupt stab of pain caused Vilém to wince.

"Ouch!" cried Raya, who was sitting on the edge of her bed. Vilém almost felt embarrassed when he realized that a mere prick from a needle had caused the sudden sting. Mrs. Pomnenka's hand had slipped while she was trying to sew something onto her daughter's dress.

"I'm sorry, darling," said Raya's mother, pursing her lips and carefully completing her work.

Raya hopped off her bed and made her way to the mirror. Vilém noticed that the lavender walls of the girl's bedroom had been almost completely covered with hundreds of black-and-white pictures. He could hardly imagine how much film the little photographer went through in a year.

He wasn't allowed to focus on the photos for too long, however, as Raya stepped in front of the mirror.

No longer was she the bright-eyed little girl that had twirled in front of the mirror on her ninth Hanukkah. Now her chestnut eyes were dimmed with dejection, most of her childish freckles had abandoned her cheeks, and a tattered, pale-blue dress was draped over her lanky thirteen-year-old frame. Her auburn hair was no longer tied into girlish pigtails but hung freely, without a ribbon or braid to restrain it. She had grown into a glum, pretty girl.

And the current cause of her gloominess was obvious. On the breast of her dress, right above her heart, was a yellow patch. It was a six-pointed star, and in the center of the star was a single word, written in black ink.

JEW

Mrs. Pomnenka moved to stand behind her rigid daughter, putting a hand on her head.

"There," she said, gently stroking her daughter's hair. "Not so bad. A bright, golden star. Just like you, Raya."

"It's yellow," said Raya, her bottom lip trembling. Vilém could feel dread ballooning in Raya's chest.

"Raya…"

"It's yellow and it's ugly and I hate it!" the girl squeaked, biting down on her tongue, forcing a sob to stay in her throat. "N-nobody's gonna want to talk to me…"

Mrs. Pomnenka's smile fell away and her lips tightened. She moved her hands to Raya's shoulders and squeezed tightly, as if she was trying to transfer some of her strength into the scrawny body of her daughter.

"Listen here, Raya," she whispered. "If someone won't talk to you because of that star, well, they aren't worth talking to. The Nazis are making us wear these stars so they know who we are. We mustn't be ashamed to show who we are. Wear the star with your head held high, Raya."

The girl stared at her reflection, at the star that had become the focal point of her being. Although dismay had not abandoned her heart, a small spark of pride joined it and the two sentiments began to banter over the girl's emotional state.

Finally, pride gained the upper hand long enough to convince Raya to wriggle out of her mother's grasp and run to her nightstand. Her camera was patiently resting there, waiting to capture another memory that Raya could add to her bedroom walls.

She grabbed the machine and darted back to the mirror. Keeping her elbows out so that the star would show in the picture, she lifted up the camera.

C*LICK!*

Once more, the memory dissolved into darkness.

"And then what happened?" asked Vilém when a few moments passed and no new memory cleared the gloom away.

Reinhard Heydrich happened.

"Heydrich!" Vilém exclaimed. "The Hangman of Prague!"

I figured you'd know about him.

"Ha! I failed history class, but they made sure even a piss-poor student like me left school knowing that Heydrich was a monster. I went to Prague once. I stood where he was killed. It felt...odd...angry almost. Like he was still there."

I wouldn't be surprised. Heydrich was an evil man, an arrogant man. He must still be mad about getting killed by a bunch of "inferior" Czechs. He became the Reichsprotektor of

Czechoslovakia in 1941, about a month after they forced us to wear the stars. He was brutal.

"And in 1942...the Czechs finally got sick of him."

He prodded the lion. It bit off his hand.

"But what does Heydrich have to do with your story?"

The Nazis weren't happy that a gang of Czechs assassinated their top man, and they made sure we all paid for it.

"Right, I remember that. They completely destroyed a Czech village somewhere...Lidice, I think it was called."

You're right again. They destroyed Lidice as part of their revenge, but only part. They also deported hundreds of Jews, including me.

"Get up!"

A shout caused the darkness to stir. Vilém felt Raya's heart lurch as her eyelids fluttered open and she saw her mother standing above her.

Raya's vision was hazy from fatigue. Her mother's face was foggy, so foggy that Vilém could hardly tell what expression she was wearing. Judging purely by her frantic tone, however, he could deduce that something was horribly wrong. The exhausted Raya could apparently tell as well. Her pulse started to race with worry.

"M-Mama...?"

Before Raya could ask any questions, Mrs. Pomnenka grabbed the groggy girl by the arm and yanked her out of bed. Raya nearly tripped as her mother dragged her out of the room.

"Mama!"

"We have to go now!"

"Mama, my camera!" cried Raya, her bleary vision beginning to clear as her mother yanked her down the stairs.

"We don't have time, Raya! We have to go *now!*"

Mrs. Pomnenka threw the front door open and Raya shivered. It was almost dawn, and the air was still crisp and cold. Wearing nothing but a nightgown, Raya felt the breeze bite at her flesh. Confusion, discomfort, and fear whirled about in her mind like items swept up in a tornado.

"Where's Papa?"

"He went out! We'll have to find him later!"

"But...!"

Raya stopped speaking as her mother pulled her out of the house and they ran down the street. She could hear glass shattering, children crying, horrible screams. The smell of smoke drifted through the air. She saw people lying on the streets in fetal positions as black-garbed men with truncheons beat them. She saw soldiers dragging writhing people away. She saw houses on fire, houses that Vilém could only assume belonged to Jews.

The sun was peeking out over the horizon, as though curious about the hubbub down below. A lovely assortment of orange and red hues were splashed across the sky. It was a beautiful sunrise, a beautiful morning, and Vilém could tell that Raya would like nothing more than to walk back home, sit on her porch, and watch the sun wake up. Maybe even take some pictures.

But when she dared to look over her shoulder, dared to glance back at her precious house, she saw fire spreading across the roof. Sadness stabbed at her heart. She no doubt realized that her beloved home would soon be nothing more than a singed shell.

Raya wasn't given much time to dwell upon her

house's demise. As soon as she turned towards her mother, something smacked her on the back of the head.

She fell to the concrete, her head throbbing, stars dancing in front of her eyes. From above, she heard a scream.

"Mama..." Raya mumbled as Mrs. Pomnenka's fingers were wrenched from her wrist. The girl tried to sit up, but her efforts were rewarded with another strike to her skull.

She lay on the street, barely able to look up. Her vision cleared just enough for her to see a man in black kick her mother's head.

"Mama..." Raya moaned pitifully, her head pounding with pain, her limbs heavy as iron weights. She heard two unfamiliar voices above her talking in an alien tongue. Vilém immediately realized they were speaking German, and while he was by no means fluent in the foreign language, he could pick out a few words.

"Girl...Jew...small, but healthy...camp..."

After they came to an agreement of some sort, they yanked the girl to her feet. Raya, terribly dizzy and terribly confused, shook her head to banish the bleariness from her eyes.

She saw her mother on the ground, trying to crawl towards her daughter despite her hands being covered in blood and punctured with broken glass. She saw the SS officer shove her mama against a wall.

"M..."

But before the word could even escape her lips, before Mrs. Pomnenka could even hope to run, the Nazi took out his gun.

BANG!

And when he fired, the memory didn't melt. It shattered.

All of Raya's shock, pain, anguish, and anger hit Vilém like a massive wave, melding with his own emotions until he felt like they *were* his own. Until he felt like he had just witnessed *his* mother's death.

"N-no!"

The void was gone, the shattered memory was gone, and he was standing in the middle of Barrack Five once more. His whole body was shaking, coated in sticky sweat, and his heart was beating so fast that he had to put his hand over his breast and breathe slowly to steady it.

Calm, he commanded his frenzied pulse. *Calm...calm...*

The frantic beat died down and he wiped the sweat from his brow. He was still quivering, and his hand felt like he had shoved it into a bucket of snow.

My hand...

He looked back up at the wall, at the twenty-four *Raya Pomnenkas*. He had been so overwhelmed by Raya's agony that he had taken his hand off the wall, yanked himself out of her memory.

And part of him wanted to stay out. That last memory had been too brutal, too much for him to handle. He didn't want to go back and feel the pain of the tormented spirit. He didn't want to see anymore.

But he could still sense her. He could sense Raya's spirit lingering by the letters, anxiously awaiting his return. He couldn't let her down now. He couldn't leave her to suffer alone. As much as he wanted to walk away, he needed to stay.

His legs sluggishly protested, but eventually his determined mind convinced his limbs to haul him back to the wall. He lifted his cold, heavy arm and placed his hand against the jagged letters. Vilém took a deep breath, bracing himself for the impending sorrow, and shut his eyes.

Darkness greeted him. Then, a voice.

You came back.

"I...I'm sorry. About your mother...and about leaving. I was..."

You came back. That's what matters. Thank you.

"What happened after...that?"

I was put on a train...

"Your father...?"

I never saw him again.

"I...I'm very sorry..."

You didn't do it.

"So you were all by yourself...and the train..."

It took me right to the Camp, the one you're guarding now. Of course, the guards back then...they weren't as good as you.

"Well," said Vilém, finding an almost morbid urge to chuckle, "I would think not."

We got to the Camp, me and the other Jews, and the Selection started.

Vilém didn't need to ask what the Selection was. He had spent enough hours at the Camp reading the educational placards to know what happened to the new arrivals once they reached their destination. The Selection meant either slave labor or death.

And in Raya's case, the Selection meant fogginess. At least it seemed that way when the memory finally materialized. It took a moment for Vilém to realize that the weather wasn't the cause of the hazy cloud that had descended upon Raya's recollection. Without her camera, Raya's memory was fuzzy. Faces were blurry, sounds distorted, and a strange mist was covering the whole campground.

"It's hard to see..." Vilém commented, focusing as hard as he could on the few spots of complete clarity.

I'm sorry. Like I said, my memory's always been bad. It's been so long, and without my camera...

"Don't apologize, Raya. I understand."

Raya was roughly shoved to the front of the winding line that had formed. She gazed up at the SS guard in charge of the Selection, who had been rendered faceless by the fog.

"Age?" he asked, his voice echoing about the memory.

"Sixteen." She was stifling a sob. He could feel her heart sitting at the bottom of her stomach, too heavy to lift itself back up to its rightful place.

"Scrawny," the Nazi observed, a hint of malice coming to his strange voice. "Do you have any special skills? Useful skills?"

Raya swallowed and stayed silent for a moment.

"Right. Well..."

"I can develop..."

The Nazi, clearly angered about being interrupted, barked, "What?"

"I can develop photos. I'm a photographer."

The fog cleared away from the lower half of the SS guard's face, revealing a wide smirk.

"Well!" he exclaimed. He looked over at another featureless SS man and shouted something in German. Vilém caught the word "Kommandant."

"Kommandant?" Vilém repeated as the guard yanked Raya out of line. The frightened girl didn't struggle as the Nazis took her from her fellow Jews and pulled her towards Barrack One, the Kommandant's barrack.

A fellow photographer.

The memory shifted suddenly. Raya was standing in a well-furnished office. The mist of forgetfulness had noticeably cleared, though the Nazi that stood beside her remained faceless.

However, another Nazi, one with more medals and patches decorating his dark uniform, stood before her. His face and voice were clear as day: blonde hair, blue eyes, the ideal Aryan. He smiled down at the girl, his sapphire irises twinkling.

"Be that the case, Little Jewess..." the Kommandant said.

"Raya..." the girl whispered. "Raya. My name is Raya Pomnenka."

The Kommandant's dark blue eyes flashed with amusement.

"Is that your price?" he asked. Raya felt a twinge of confusion, but she didn't respond.

"Fine then," said the Kommandant. "You won't get a number like the others, *Raya*. I have to say, you're very lucky I found you. I've been waiting forever to find somebody who loves photography as much as I do. If you can develop and develop well, you'll be perfectly fine."

He had sensitive skin, sensitive eyes, a sensitive nose...at least when it came to developing chemicals, so he never learned to develop the photos he took.

"What sort of...photos?" asked Vilém while the memory trickled into oblivion.

BARRACK FIVE

He couldn't stand the smell of chemicals. Corpses, on the other hand...well, he couldn't get enough of those. At least as long as they were Jews...

The abyss that followed the last memory twisted itself into a new recollection. Raya was standing in a dark, stuffy room, her hands stinging from the chemicals she was using to develop the photos. The Kommandant had given her thin, tattered gloves that hardly protected her flesh from the burning liquid.

Raya, though, scarcely seemed to notice the pain. She hung a newly developed photo up on a wire where it could properly dry. Her eyes darted from picture to picture and Vilém felt her stomach coil in disgust as she saw what moments in time the Kommandant had been so keen to capture.

The crowded Selection platform. Men, women, and little children crying as the SS guards shoved them into line.

The train that had transported the Jews to the Camp.

The boxcars filled with the bodies of those who hadn't survived the long journey.

Prisoners lined up outside for roll call, shivering as snow fell upon them. Their thin black-and-white uniforms couldn't hope to keep them warm in such weather.

A prisoner dangling limply from a piano wire. He must have broken one of the Camp's many rules. His executioner, a young SS guard, seemed proud of his handiwork. The youthful killer posed by the body and smiled at the camera.

Emaciated prisoners lifting heavy bags of sand. It was a wonder that their skeletal frames could support their own scant weight, much less that of a burdensome bag.

A man tangled in the electrified barbed wire that surrounded the Camp. Perhaps he had been trying to escape, or perhaps he had merely wanted to end it quickly. Either way, his scorched corpse hung lifelessly on the wire, like a ragdoll that had been carelessly tossed onto the fence.

Raya's gut roiled violently, but she refused to vomit. She didn't want to end up like the people featured in the Kommandant's photographs. She had to keep going.

She tugged on her frayed gloves and got started on the next picture.

The memory faded.

"Why...?" Vilém started to ask, woozy with nausea. "Why would the Kommandant take pictures like that?"

Same reason I did, I suppose. Memories. He wanted to remember all of his...achievements. Funny thing is, I remember he had a son, a sweet little boy, but he never took pictures of him growing up. I think I only ever developed three pictures of his child. I guess the Kommandant didn't want to waste film on his own son when there were so many miserable Jews to photograph.

"Those pictures...the pictures of the Camp...I think some of them are in the exhibit."

Exhibit?

"For the museum, for the Camp. I didn't know you developed them."

Raya was silent for a moment.

"Raya?"

I developed all the Kommandant's pictures. I worked for him for two years, until 1944.

"What happened then?"

The war. The war started to get bad for the Germans. They started getting worried. Worried they would lose, and worried that once they lost and everyone found out what they did...well, you understand. The Kommandant stopped photographing his work.

A new memory appeared. Raya's heart was pounding so loudly that it almost gave Vilém a headache. The girl was crouching by the door of the Kommandant's office, peeking inside.

The Kommandant had placed his camera on the floor. He looked down at the machine, his eyes shimmering with fearful regret. He took a deep breath and raised his foot over the device.

The Nazi's steel-lined boot crushed the camera, smashing its lens and causing bits of metal to scatter across the floor. Raya whimpered and began to tremble in terror, no doubt realizing that, with the camera's destruction, the Kommandant no longer needed a developer.

The memory dissolved.

The Kommandant stopped taking pictures, and he also stopped giving me special treatment. A few weeks later, he transferred me to Barrack Five. I never saw him again, but I know he bit down on a cyanide pill just as the Russians made it to the Camp. Never got interrogated. Never got punished.

"What happened to you, though?" asked Vilém.

After the Nazis moved me to Barrack Five, they gave me a new assignment. I was to clean the latrines.

As soon as he heard the word "latrines", Vilém braced himself for sludge. He was tossed into another memory and an atrocious stench promptly assaulted his sinuses.

Raya was kneeling down before a toilet, her fingers covered in filth. She was forced to reach in and scoop out the muck with her bare hands. Vilém squirmed with disgust as he felt the grime stick to the girl's skin. He felt anger and humiliation burn in Raya's chest as she listened to her supervising SS officer laugh at her.

Vilém was more than grateful when the memory dissipated.

"Revolting," he commented.

And unsanitary. You can imagine doing that every day without ever really washing or wearing gloves...

"You'd get sick...." Vilém muttered, his stomach sinking with dread when he realized what was about to happen.

I did.

Slowly, the shadows that surrounded him morphed into a new memory.

Heavy. Her body felt heavy. Her arms and legs felt like they were made of bricks rather than flesh and blood. Her bones felt like they had been encased in steel, rendered far too cumbersome for her to lift.

She was lying on the rough wooden plank of her bunk, watching as the last prisoner left Barrack Five to report for roll call. Raya Pomnenka whimpered. Her fingers twitched and she tried to reach for her fellow prisoners, tried to beg for their help, but her throat was too dry. Water. She wanted just a sip of cold water to soothe her arid throat.

But more than that, she wanted a hand to hold, an ear to whisper a few last words into. She didn't want to die here. She didn't want to die like this. Sick, silent, alone.

She could feel her spirit slipping out of her body, as if

she had been shot and her blood was slowly draining away, leaving only her lifeless corpse behind. She frantically tried to keep the Grim Reaper at bay, to get his cold, clammy hands off of her.

Yet Death refused to yield. She looked up at the wall beside her and tried to lift her arm, tried to touch the wall. It was her last desperate deed. Vilém could tell right away what she wanted to do.

But she didn't have the strength to write her name on the wall of Barrack Five. Her arm fell to her side and she wanted to cry, but she wasn't even strong enough to shed a tear.

The barrack became blurry, the dull colors fused together to form an appalling blob of brown and gray, and the very last thing that Raya Pomnenka felt was a horrible mixture of loneliness and regret.

Darkness.

Vilém opened his eyes.

He felt cold, numb, as though he too had been embraced by the Grim Reaper's icy arms. Yet he felt his heart beating, he felt his blood slowly warm and rush through his veins, and he had never been more grateful to feel his soul resting securely within his functioning body.

He looked at the words on the wall, the twenty-four *Raya Pomnenkas* that the spirit had carved so anxiously, and he understood.

Raya Pomnenka's hometown had been destroyed, her parents had been killed, everything she had ever known had been wiped out. And on top of all that, everything that had ever known *her* had been obliterated.

The Kommandant had died before he could tell

anyone about the girl who had developed his morbid pictures. Her parents had died before they could tell the world about their beloved daughter. Her classmates and neighbors had died before they could utter a word about her. All of the pictures she had taken, all of her memories, had been destroyed the same day she had been shipped to the Camp.

There was no diary of Raya Pomnenka that hundreds of people could read. There was no memoir about her sitting on a library shelf. She didn't even get her name inscribed on a commemorative plaque.

It was as though she had never even lived. The Nazis had taken her home, her family, her pictures, her very name, and they had all but taken away her existence.

The carvings on the wall were a desperate effort to exist, to make sure somebody, anybody, at least knew her name. To make sure she didn't completely fade into oblivion.

Vilém clenched his jaw. As far as he was concerned, the girl deserved better than this. She deserved more than graffiti on a barrack wall. She deserved a plaque at least. He would have to work something out, talk to his boss, see what he could manage. Of course, he could hardly say that the ghost of the girl who had developed the pictures displayed in the museum's exhibit had come to him and told him her tale. But no matter what, he would find a way to share the spirit's name and tell her story.

For now, though, he was exhausted and rather depressed. He needed to go home and start planning.

But before he did that, he looked back up at the twenty-four *Raya Pomnenkas*. He could still sense the spirit's cold presence close by. She had something else to say.

He placed his hand on the markings and closed his eyes.

Vilém...

"Yes, Raya?"

Can...I ask you something?

"Of course, Raya."

Will you remember me?

Without a moment of hesitation, he replied, "Of course, Raya. I'll always remember you."

Raya Pomnenka's icy aura became warm as a ray of sun. Slowly, he felt her fade away.

No more markings appeared on the wall of Barrack Five.

AFTERWORD

Thank you for reading Barrack Five!
The sequel, Barrack Four, is available right now!
If you would like to read more stories like this one,
follow Project 613 on Twitter @Project613Books, on
Facebook, and sign up for updates at Project613Publishing.com!

Made in the USA
Columbia, SC
12 July 2025